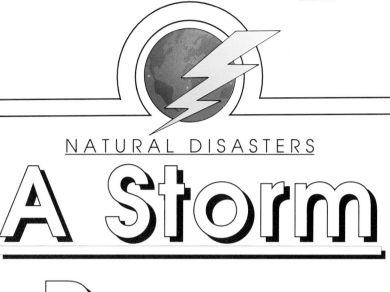

NATURAL DISASTERS

A Storm Rages

Susan Bullen

Wayland

Natural Disasters

A Storm Rages
A Volcano Erupts
Flood Damage
The Power of
Earthquakes

Editor: Deb Elliott
Designer: Malcolm Walker

Cover pictures: background – Lightning
strikes. left – A lightning storm rages over
Colorado in the USA. middle – A scene of
devastation in Cutler Ridge, Florida after
Hurricane Andrew struck in August 1992.
right – A tropical storm seen from space.
This storm caused serious damage on the
Hawaiian island of Kauai in September
1992.

Text is based on *Storm* in *The Violent Earth*
series published in 1992

First published in 1994 by
Wayland (Publishers) Ltd
61 Western Road, Hove
East Sussex, BN3 1JD, England

**British Library Cataloguing in Publication
Data**
Bullen, Susan
  Storm rages. - (Natural Disasters Series)
  I. Title II. Series
  551.55

ISBN 0 7502 1189 X

Typeset by Kudos
Printed and bound by
  Rotolito Lombarda s.p.a.

J551·55

Contents

◄ *A dark, stormy sky at Sidmouth beach in Devon, England.*

A storm disaster

Look at all the broken wood in the photograph below. The wood used to be people's homes until a storm came and blew it all down.

▼ *The damage was caused by a storm called a cyclone.*

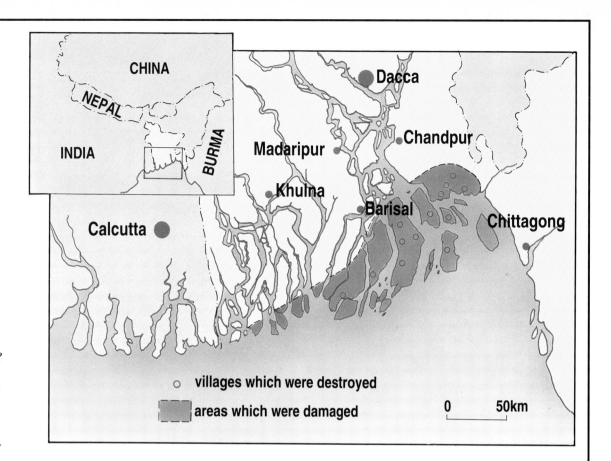

This is where damage from the cyclone took place. ▶

villages which were destroyed

areas which were damaged

0   50km

Storms are very dangerous

Cyclones are storms with very strong winds. They happen in tropical countries.

The cyclone hit Bangladesh, near India, in November 1970. Strong winds turned the sea wild. A giant wave higher than a house rolled over low-lying land in Bangladesh. It ruined people's homes and their crops. About 150,000 people died and thousands of animals were killed too.

Many kinds of storms

Cyclones are one kind of storm. There are also rainstorms, snowstorms, sandstorms and thunderstorms. Have you seen a thunderstorm? When it begins, the sky fills with dark clouds and the air feels very heavy. There is a flash of lightning followed by rumbling thunder. Then it often pours with rain.

▼   *This is a thunderstorm in Arizona, USA. Look at the lightning flashing across the black sky.*

The weather makes storms

In some countries the weather is always changing. One day can be hot and the next day can be cold. It can be windy or still and wet or dry.

▼ *This picture shows how rain falls to the ground and how clouds form again.*

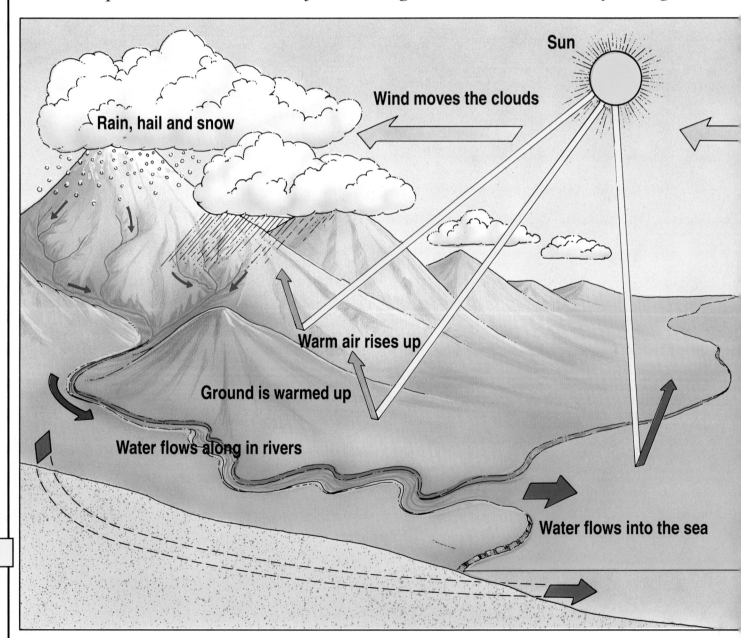

Sun

Wind moves the clouds

Rain, hail and snow

Warm air rises up

Ground is warmed up

Water flows along in rivers

Water flows into the sea

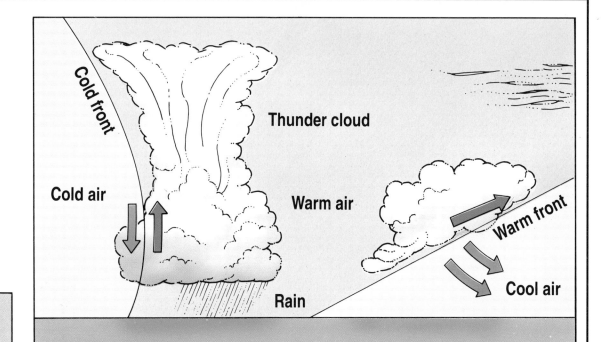

Thunder cloud

Cold front

Cold air

Warm air

Warm front

Cool air

Rain

→ Warm air
⇒ Cold air

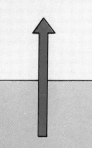

Wetness in the air turns into cloud

Tiny droplets of water go from the sea into the air

▲ *Storms can occur when warm and cold air meet above the Earth.*

Clouds form along the edges between warm air and cold air. They are called warm and cold fronts. ▶

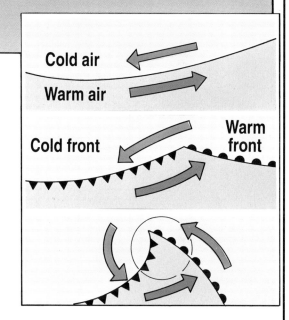

Cold air

Warm air

Cold front

Warm front

The weather changes because the air temperature changes. The Sun's heat warms the Earth and the air around it. Warm air rises and then cold air fills the space lower down. Warm and cold air masses swirl around the Earth but do not mix.

Thunderstorms

▼ *Thunderstorms happen all over the world. The diagram below shows how they work.*

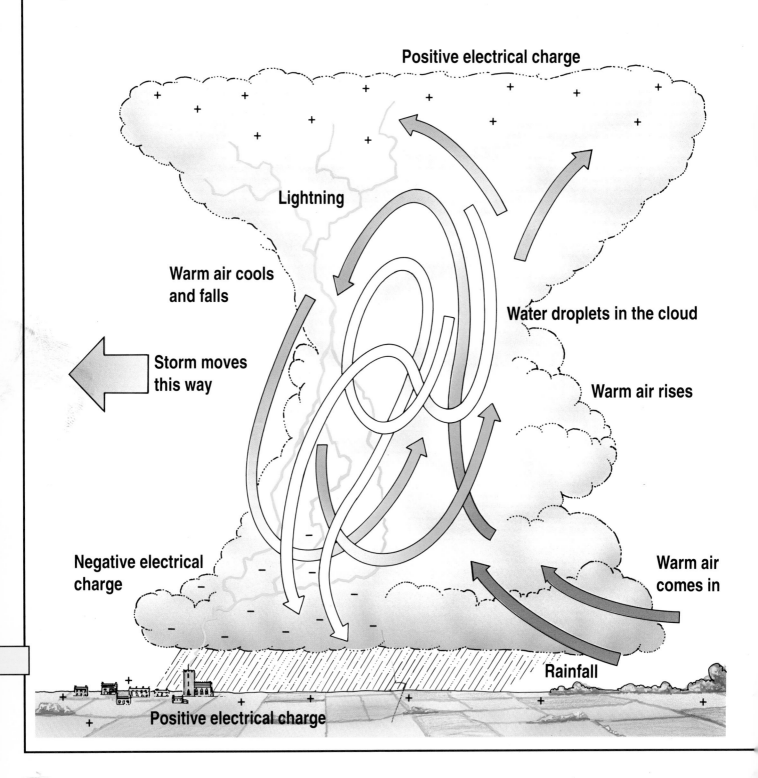

Positive electrical charge

Lightning

Warm air cools and falls

Storm moves this way

Water droplets in the cloud

Warm air rises

Negative electrical charge

Warm air comes in

Rainfall

Positive electrical charge

▲ *Thunder and lightning happen together, but we see the flash before we hear the rumble.*

Inside a thundercloud, air moves around very fast and throws water droplets and ice around. Electrical charges build up and burst out of the cloud as lightning. As hot lightning touches cool air, it makes the loud noise we call thunder.

Snowstorms

Do you like snow? It only happens when the air temperature is lower than 4°C. Snow is made when cold air comes over from the polar regions and meets with warm air, forming snow clouds.

Snow falls in cooler countries but also in warmer countries on high mountains.

▼ *Look how snow is made.*

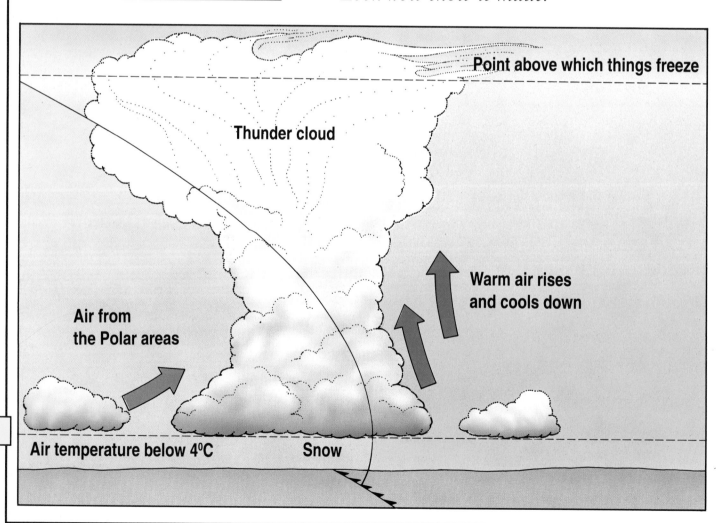

Point above which things freeze

Thunder cloud

Warm air rises and cools down

Air from the Polar areas

Air temperature below 4⁰C   Snow

◄ *A snowflake is made of tiny ice crystals. Each flake has a pretty pattern.*

A blanket of snow looks pretty, but it can bury cars and animals. Strong snowstorms are called blizzards. They are very dangerous.

▼ *A snow plough clears snow from this road in the USA so cars can get by.*

Dust storms and sandstorms

Dust storms happen in dry places where few plants grow. When a strong wind comes, it blows the dry, dusty soil around. The air becomes thick with dust.

The Dust Bowl

In the 1930s a disaster hit midwestern USA. The weather was hot and dry for so long that the soil turned to dust. In 1934 and 1935 big winds made dust storms. Farmers could not grow wheat any more, and thousands of people left their homes and moved away. The area became known as the Dust Bowl.

In the 1930s a huge part of the USA dried out and turned to dust. People called it the Dust Bowl. The photograph below shows a family praying for the rain to come and wash away the dust.

Sandstorms

Sandstorms are like dust storms of the desert. Strong winds blow the dry sand around. It stings people's faces and they cannot see where they are going.

▼   *These people in Cameroon, Africa, are crossing the desert in a sandstorm.*

Tornadoes

Have you seen the wind chasing fallen leaves in a circle? That is like a small whirlwind. A tornado is a very strong whirlwind that spins around very fast. Tornadoes can travel at 100 kilometres per hour. They wreck homes and blow down trees.

◄ *This is a tornado. The whirling wind makes a funnel-shaped cloud.*

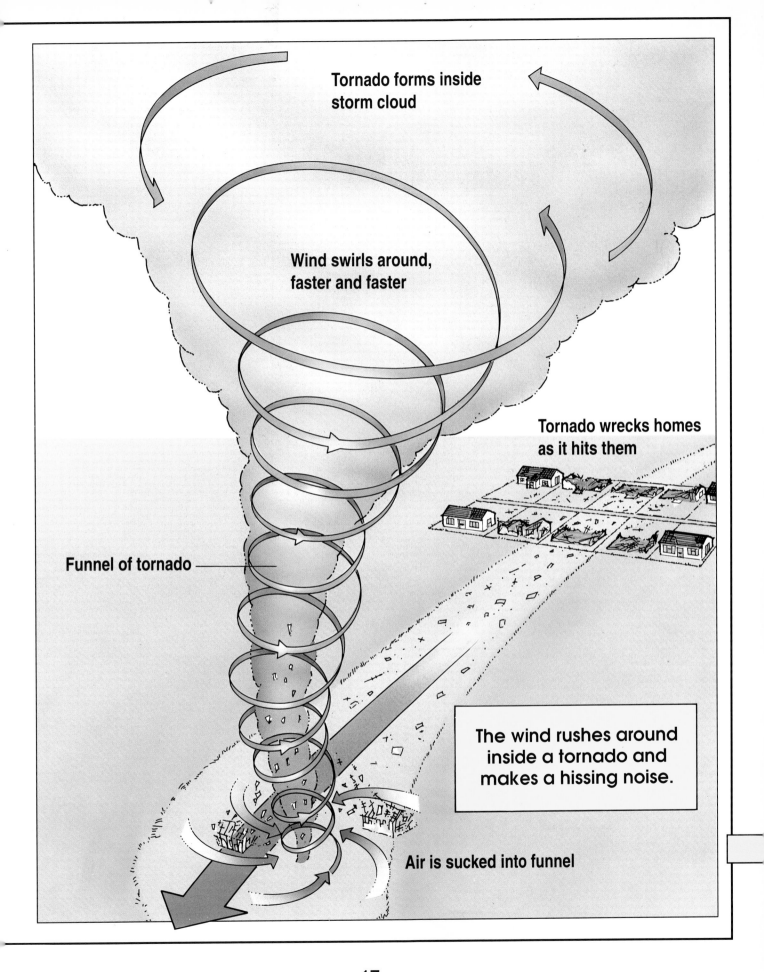

Tornado forms inside storm cloud

Wind swirls around, faster and faster

Tornado wrecks homes as it hits them

Funnel of tornado

The wind rushes around inside a tornado and makes a hissing noise.

Air is sucked into funnel

Many tornadoes happen in the USA, usually in spring. In April 1974, over 100 tornadoes hit the USA in only two days. They killed 300 people and damaged many towns and villages.

▼ *Look at these homes. They were ruined by a tornado.*

Tornadoes blow down trees and strip off their bark and leaves. They can even tear off people's clothes.

People at American weather stations are always on the look-out for tornadoes. If a tornado is on its way, there are warnings on television and radio. They give people some time to get away from danger.

Hurricanes

Hurricanes are even bigger and stronger than tornadoes. These terrifying winds start as big clouds over the sea. As they move in to the land, they cause devastation. Hurricanes happen in many parts of the world, even in Europe. They rip down trees and houses and cause chaos everywhere.

These are hurricane clouds. They swirl around the calm ring in the centre, called the eye. ▶

A hurricane forms over the sea. Clouds build up as warm air rises and cold air rushes in to take its place. ▶

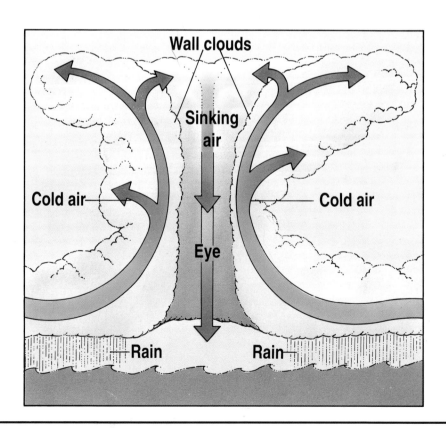

Famous hurricanes which have happened in the USA

Date	Place	People killed
1900	Galveston, Texas	6000
1928	Lake Okeechobee, Florida	1800
1957	Louisiana, Mississippi and Texas	550
1969	Louisiana to Virginia	250
1972	Florida to New York	122
1983	Galveston, Texas	21

Storm damage

Storms of some kind happen in most parts of the world. The USA has hurricanes, tornadoes, dust storms, snowstorms and rainstorms.

▼ *Stormy winds blew down these trees in an American town.*

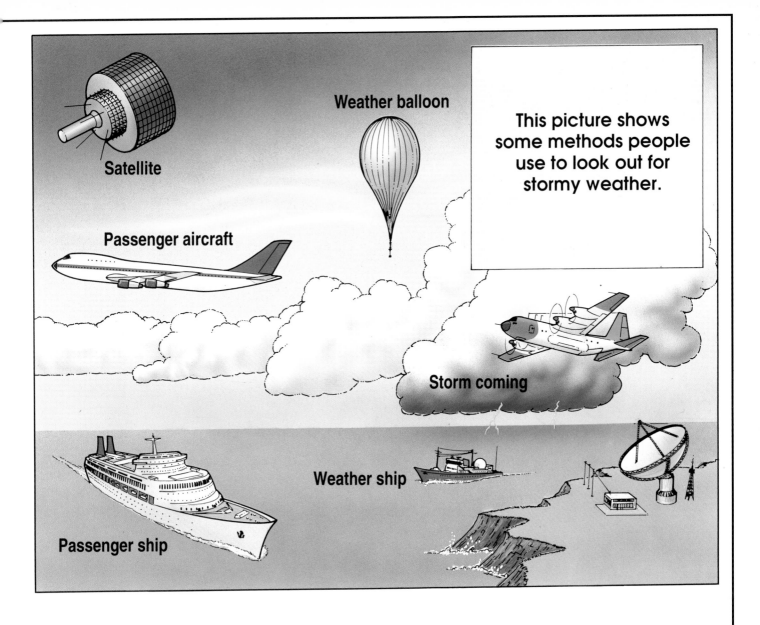

Satellite

Weather balloon

This picture shows some methods people use to look out for stormy weather.

Passenger aircraft

Storm coming

Weather ship

Passenger ship

Storms are less dangerous if people have time to get away. In many parts of the world, weather forecasters watch out for storms. They use aeroplanes, balloons, ships and satellites to watch the sky.

In poorer, tropical countries, many people cannot escape from storms. Often they have houses which are easily damaged. Low-lying places like Bangladesh and the Philippine Islands often have terrible floods after storms.

▼ *A satellite picture of a swirling cyclone.*

▼ *This man and his wife lost their home when a hurricane blew into Central America. The hurricane was called Hurricane Fifi.*

Imagine if a storm did this to your home.

Can we stop storms?

All around the world, weather forecasters are watching for storms. They receive information from weather stations, weather ships and planes. Weather satellites fly around high above the Earth. They take pictures of the clouds in the sky. These pictures show how storms are moving around the world.

◀ *Weather scientists in Canada measure the wind speed.*

▲ *This weather forecaster is using computers to watch the world's weather.*

Once weather forecasters know where a storm is going, they can warn people who are in danger. We cannot stop bad storms, but we can warn people and save many lives.

Projects

Make an electric charge

Lightning happens when electric charges build up in the air. Try this experiment to see how it works.

What to do:

1 Cut the paper into small pieces.
2 Rub the comb briskly over the cloth.
3 Hold the comb over the pieces of paper. What happens?

The pieces of paper have become positively charged. The comb now has a negative charge. These opposite charges are attracted to each other and so the paper moves to the comb.

You need:
a comb
a piece of paper
scissors
a piece of woollen or
nylon cloth

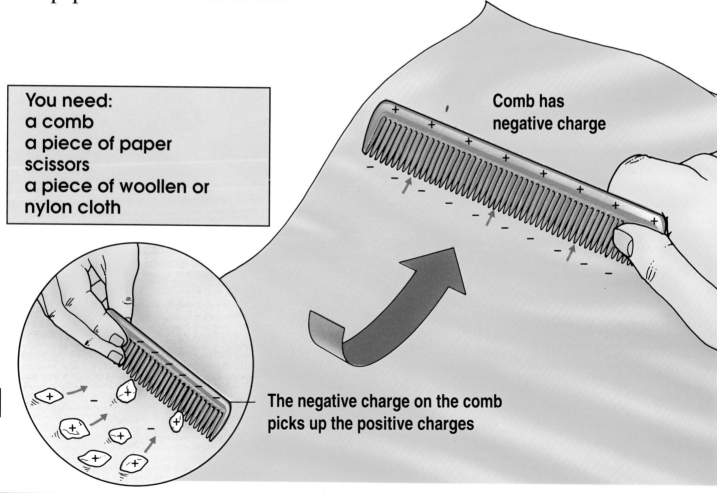

Comb has
negative charge

The negative charge on the comb
picks up the positive charges

Measure the wind speed

What to do:

1   Cut three long strips of paper, all the same length. Roll them into tubes. Make a shorter, fatter paper tube too.

2   Put the plate on to the card and draw around it. Cut out this circle and stick on the fat tube in the centre.

3   Tape each long tube to a jar lid. Now use tape to stick the three tubes evenly on to the card circle.

4   Stick a strip of red paper on to one of the lids.

5   Push the pencil into the short middle tube. When you turn the pencil, the card should spin around.

6   Now go outside and hold your machine into the wind. Count how often the red strip goes by in 1 minute.

You need:
a piece of card
a small plate
a pencil
scissors
strong paper and card
3 jar tops
sticky tape
a strip of red paper

Wind

Card
Short tube
Lids

Red strip
of paper

Sticky
tape

Tubes of
rolled-up
paper

Glossary

air temperature   How hot or cold the air is.

cause   Make happen.

cyclone   A strong, windy storm in hot parts of the world.

eye   The calm ring in the centre of hurricane clouds.

satellite   An instrument that flies around above the Earth.

tropical countries   Countries that are found each side of the Equator.

weather forecasters   People who study the weather and say what will happen.

whirlwind   A wind that blows in a circle.

Books to read

Storms by Philip Steele
 (Franklin Watts, 1991)
Storms by Jenny Wood
 (Franklin Watts, 1990)
The Weather in Winter by Miriam Moss
 (Wayland, 1994)

Picture acknowledgements
The publisher would like to thank the following for allowing their photographs to be reproduced in this book: Camera Press 4 (Gus Coral); the Hutchison Library (Val & Alan Wilkinson) 14/15; J. Allan Cash Ltd 2/3; Frank Lane Picture Agency 22; Rex Features (Matthew Naythons/Sipa Press) 25; 6/7 (Ken Wood), 11 (Gordon Gerradd), 21 (Hasler & Pierce NASA GSFC), 24 (NOAA), 26 (Stephen Krasemann); Science Photo Library cover (left, Keith Kent) (right, NASA); Frank Spooner cover (middle, GAMMA LIAISON); Tony Stone Worldwide cover (background, Ralph Wetmore), 13 (bottom); Topham Picture Library 14 (bottom), 16; Zefa Picture Library 13 top (Dr F. Sauer), 18/19. 27 (B. Harris).

Index